THE MIDNIGHT ADVENTURE OF KATE SHELLEY,

TRAIN RESCUER

BY **MARGARET K. WETTERER**
ADAPTED BY **EMMA CARLSON BERNE**
ILLUSTRATED BY **ZACHARY TROVER**

INTRODUCTION

KATHERINE CARROLL SHELLEY WAS BORN IN IRELAND ON SEPTEMBER 25, 1865. HER FAMILY CALLED HER KATE. BEFORE SHE WAS A YEAR OLD, HER PARENTS BROUGHT HER TO AMERICA. THEY BOUGHT A SMALL FARM NEAR THE TOWN OF MOINGONA, IOWA. KATE'S FATHER BUILT A HOUSE OVERLOOKING HONEY CREEK, WITHIN SIGHT OF THE CHICAGO AND NORTHWESTERN RAILROAD LINE, AND FARMED THE LAND. HE ALSO TOOK A JOB WITH THE RAILROAD. AFTER KATE, THERE WERE FOUR MORE CHILDREN, JAMES, MAYME, MARGARET, AND JOHN. LIFE IN THE SHELLEYS' ISOLATED COTTAGE WAS HARD BUT FULL OF GOOD FRIENDS AND GOOD TIMES.

THEN, WHEN KATE WAS 13, HER FATHER DIED. LESS THAN ONE YEAR
LATER, 10-YEAR-OLD JAMES DROWNED IN THE DES MOINES RIVER.
MRS. SHELLEY NEVER REALLY RECOVERED FROM THESE TRAGEDIES.
KATE TOOK OVER MORE AND MORE RESPONSIBILITY FOR RUNNING
THE FARM AND FOR CARING FOR THE YOUNGER CHILDREN.

IN 1881, A RAGING STORM HIT THE DES MOINES RIVER VALLEY. KATE
KNEW THAT LIVES COULD BE LOST. BUT SHE DID NOT HESITATE TO FACE
DANGER AND GO OUT ALONE INTO THE NIGHT TO DO WHAT SHE BELIEVED
WAS HER DUTY.

MOINGONA, IOWA
JULY 6, 1881
KATE! HURRY! A BAD STORM IS COMING!
I'M COMING, MOTHER. I JUST HAVE TO GET THE SHEETS IN.
RRRRUMMMBLE
RRRRUMMMBLE

HELP US!

HANG ON! HANG ON! I'M GOING TO GET HELP.

KATE HAD TO GET TO THE STATION BEFORE MIDNIGHT, BEFORE THE EXPRESS. SHE HAD TO CROSS THE DES MOINES RIVER.

CREAK

CREAK

KATE CAREFULLY MADE HER WAY OVER THE LARGE GAPS BETWEEN THE BRIDGE'S PLANKS.

Des Moines River Bridge

CLANK!

THE TREE SCRAPED THE SUPPORTS AS IT PASSED, BUT THE BRIDGE HELD.

I MUST KEEP GOING. IT'S ALMOST MIDNIGHT.

I HAVE TO REACH THE STATION BEFORE THE MIDNIGHT EXPRESS REACHES HONEY CREEK.

THE STATION WAS LESS THAN A HALF MILE AHEAD.

AFTERWORD

KATE WENT HOME AND SLEPT FOR A LONG TIME. WHEN SHE AWOKE, HER FAMILY, FRIENDS, AND NEIGHBORS GREETED HER HAPPILY. THEY WANTED TO HEAR ABOUT HER ADVENTURE. REPORTERS CAME. NEWSPAPERS ACROSS THE COUNTRY TOLD THE STORY OF HER BRAVERY. SOON THE WHOLE NATION KNEW ABOUT KATE SHELLEY. THE RAILROAD COMPANY GAVE KATE ONE HUNDRED DOLLARS AND A LIFETIME PASS ON THE RAILROAD. POEMS AND SONGS WERE WRITTEN IN HER HONOR. THE STATE OF IOWA AWARDED HER A GOLD MEDAL. THE RAILROAD COMPANY BUILT A NEW BRIDGE IN 1901 AND NAMED IT AFTER KATE.

KATE TAUGHT SCHOOL FOR MANY YEARS. IN 1903, SHE BECAME THE STATION AGENT OF THE SAME TRAIN STATION WHERE SHE GAVE HER WARNING SO MANY YEARS BEFORE. SHE CARED FOR HER MOTHER UNTIL HER MOTHER'S DEATH IN 1909. KATE DIED IN 1912.

FURTHER READING AND WEBSITES

CROWTHER, ROBERT. *TRAINS: A POP-UP RAILROAD BOOK*. CAMBRIDGE, MA: CANDLEWICK PRESS, 2006.

FARMERS AND FARM LIFE
HTTP://WWW.IPTV.ORG/IOWAPATHWAYS/MYPATH.CFM?OUNID=OB_000043

FARM WOMEN
HTTP://WWW.IPTV.ORG/IOWAPATHWAYS/MYPATH.CFM?OUNID=OB_000055

HALLEY, NED. *EYEWITNESS: FARM*. NEW YORK: DORLING KINDERSLEY, 2000.

HAZEN, WALTER A. *EVERYDAY LIFE: THE FRONTIER*. TUCSON, AZ: GOOD YEAR BOOKS, 2008.

HILL, LEE SULLIVAN. *TRAINS*. MINNEAPOLIS: LERNER PUBLICATIONS COMPANY, 2003.

KATE SHELLEY BRIDGE
HTTP://WWW.STUORG.IASTATE.EDU/RAILROAD/AMES/KATESHELLEY.HTML

LADOUX, RITA C. *IOWA*. MINNEAPOLIS: LERNER PUBLICATIONS COMPANY, 2002.

NELSON, ROBIN. *FROM CEMENT TO BRIDGE*. MINNEAPOLIS: LERNER PUBLICATIONS COMPANY, 2004.

O'BRIEN, PATRICK. *STEAM, SMOKE, AND STEEL: BACK IN TIME WITH TRAINS*. WATERTOWN, MA: CHARLESBRIDGE, 2000.

UNION PACIFIC PHOTO GALLERY
HTTP://WWW.UPRR.COM/ABOUTUP/PHOTOS/INDEX.SHTML

WILDER, LAURA INGALLS. *ON THE BANKS OF PLUM CREEK*. NEW YORK: HARPERTROPHY, 2004.

WINGET, MARY. *FLOODS*. MINNEAPOLIS: LERNER PUBLICATIONS COMPANY, 2009.

WOLFMAN, JUDY. *LIFE ON A DAIRY FARM*. MINNEAPOLIS: LERNER PUBLICATIONS COMPANY, 2004.

ABOUT THE AUTHOR

MARGARET K. WETTERER HAS WRITTEN MANY CHILDREN'S BOOKS FOR VARIOUS PUBLISHERS. SHE LIVES IN HUNTINGTON, NEW YORK.

ABOUT THE ADAPTER

EMMA CARLSON BERNE HAS WRITTEN AND EDITED MORE THAN TWO DOZEN BOOKS FOR YOUNG PEOPLE, INCLUDING BIOGRAPHIES OF SUCH DIVERSE FIGURES AS CHRISTOPHER COLUMBUS, WILLIAM SHAKESPEARE, THE HILTON SISTERS, AND SNOOP DOGG. SHE HOLDS A MASTER'S DEGREE IN COMPOSITION AND RHETORIC FROM MIAMI UNIVERSITY. BERNE LIVES IN CINCINNATI, OHIO, WITH HER HUSBAND, AARON.

ABOUT THE ILLUSTRATOR

ZACHARY TROVER HAS BEEN DRAWING SINCE HE WAS OLD ENOUGH TO HOLD A PENCIL AND HASN'T STOPPED YET. YOU CAN FIND HIM LIVING SOMEWHERE IN THE MIDWEST WITH HIS EXTREMELY PATIENT WIFE AND TWO EXTREMELY IMPATIENT DOGS.

Text copyright © 2011 by Lerner Publishing Group, Inc.
Illustrations © 2011 by Lerner Publishing Group, Inc.

Graphic Universe™ is a trademark of Lerner Publishing Group, Inc.

Graphic Universe™
A division of Lerner Publishing Group, Inc.
241 First Avenue North
Minneapolis, MN 55401 U.S.A.

Website address: www.lernerbooks.com

Library of Congress Cataloging-in-Publication Data

Wetterer, Margaret K.
    The midnight adventure of Kate Shelley, train rescuer / by Margaret K. Wetterer ; adapted by Emma Carlson Berne ; illustrated by Zachary Trover.
        p.   cm. — (History's kid heroes)
    Summary: On July 6, 1881, in Moingona, Iowa, when a ferocious storm washes out the railroad bridges, fifteen-year-old Kate Shelley risks her life to prevent a terrible train disaster.
    Includes bibliographical references.
    ISBN: 978-0-7613-6173-2 (lib. bdg. : alk. paper)
    1. Shelley, Kate—Juvenile fiction. 2. Railroad accidents—Iowa—Moingona—Juvenile fiction.
3. Shelley, Kate—Fiction. 4. Graphic novels. [1. Graphic novels. 2. Railroad accidents—Fiction.
3. Heroes—Fiction. 4. Moingona (Iowa)—History—19th century—Fiction.] I. Trover, Zachary, ill.
II. Title.
PZ7.7.W48Mid 2011
363.12'2092—dc22 [B]   2010006746

Manufactured in the United States of America
1—CG—7/15/10